Just One More!

First published in 2008
by Wayland

Text copyright © David Orme 2008
Illustration copyright © Beccy Blake 2008

Wayland
338 Euston Road
London NW1 3BH

Wayland Australia
Level 17/207 Kent Street
Sydney, NSW 2000

Series Editor: Louise John
Editor: Katie Powell
Cover design: Paul Cherrill
Design: D.R.ink
Consultant: Shirley Bickler

A CIP catalogue record for this book is available from the British Library.

ISBN 9780750254625

Printed in China

Wayland is a division of Hachette Children's Books,
an Hachette Livre UK Company

www.hachettelivre.co.uk

Just One More!

Written by David Orme
Illustrated by Beccy Blake

WAYLAND

Dad and Freddy went
to the park.

PARK

5

Freddy played on
the roundabout.

"Push harder, Dad!"
shouted Freddy.

7

hey had a game
of football.

Freddy scored two goals!

Then he went on the slide.

"Time to go home now, Freddy," said Dad.

"One more slide, please," said Freddy.

"Just one," said Dad.

Freddy slid down.

"Hurray!" he shouted.

"Come on, Freddy," said Dad.

"One more go!"
said Freddy.

"OK," said Dad, "Just one
last slide."

Freddy slid down to the
bottom again.

He loved sliding!

Freddy looked around
but Dad had gone.

He looked and looked.

19

"Hey, Freddy! Look at me!"
shouted Dad.

He came down the slide
very fast.

"Time to go, Dad,"
said Freddy.

"Just one more go!" said Dad.
"I love sliding!"

23

START READING is a series of highly enjoyable books for beginner readers. They have been carefully graded to match the Book Bands widely used in schools. This enables readers to be sure they choose books that match their own reading ability.

The Bands are:

Pink / Band 1
Red / Band 2
Yellow / Band 3
Blue / Band 4
Green / Band 5
Orange / Band 6
Turquoise / Band 7
Purple / Band 8
Gold / Band 9

START READING books can be read independently or shared with an adult. They promote the enjoyment of reading through satisfying stories supported by fun illustrations.

David Orme lives in Hampshire, England. He taught for 18 years before becoming a full-time writer. Recent books are on subjects as varied as dragons and how to be a pop star!

Beccy Blake started drawing family life when she was about Freddy's age, and has never really stopped since. Her Granny had a dog like the one in this story and Freddy is very much like her little brothers, getting up to all sorts of mischief.